THE MUMMY

BY

JANE WEBB

British Library Cataloguing-in-Publication Data
A catalogue record for this book is available from the
British Library

CONTENTS

JANE WEBB

Jane C. Webb Loudon was born in Birmingham, England in 1807. Although she was raised in luxury, Webb's father lost all his money as a result of over-speculation, before dying penniless in 1824, when Webb was only 17. She later stated that she realized that "on the winding up of his affairs it would be necessary to do something for my support. I had written a strange, wild novel, called *The Mummy*, in which I had laid the scene in the twenty-second century, and attempted to predict the state of improvement to which this country might possibly arrive."

Possibly inspired by the 1821 public unwrappings of Egyptian mummies, as well as the 1818 publication of Mary Shelley's *Frankenstein*, Webb's *The Mummy* is a fantastical, Gothic novel concerning an Egyptian mummy named Cheops who is brought back in to life in the 22nd century. It also carries a number of science-fiction themes, predicting in some detail an imagined future, and implicitly admiring the notion of scientific progress. It was published anonymously in 1827, and was well-received by contemporary reviewers.

In 1829, she published the semi-fictional *Stories of a Bride*, her second and last venture in fiction. She then turned her hand to gardening manuals, having developed an interest in gardening from her husband, an expert in the field. Webb produced a number of entry-level guides which came to be considered standard books of reference, attaining a large circulation. Indeed, within a few years Webb and her husband were the leading horticulturists of their day, including within their circle of friends Charles Dickens and William Makepeace Thackery.

In 1843, the long-ill Mr. Loudon died of lung cancer, leaving Jane with a ten-old daughter to raise. Once again, she turned to her pen to make a living. By 1848, her daughter was sixteen, and lived an extravagant lifestyle. Jane tried to make ends meet more closely for two years by working as the editor of *The Ladies Companion at Home and Abroad*. She lived out the last two years of her life without further publishing, before dying in 1858, aged 51.

THE MUMMY

JANE WEBB

NO EVENT OF any importance occurred to our travellers in the course of their aërial voyage. They were too well provided with all kinds of necessaries to have any occasion to rest by the way, and in an incredibly short space of time they were hovering over Egypt. Different, however, how different from the Egypt of the nineteenth century, was the fertile country which now lay like a map beneath their feet! Improvement had turned her gigantic steps towards its once deserted plains; Commerce had waved her magic wand; and towns and cities, manufactaries and canals, spread in all directions. No more did the Nile overflow its banks: a thousand channels were cut to receive its waters. No longer did the moving sands of the Desert rise in mighty waves, threatening to overwhelm the wayworn traveller: macadamized turnpike roads supplied their place, over which post-chaises, with anti-attritioned wheels, bowled at the rate of fifteen miles an hour. Steam boats glided down the canals, and furnaces raised their smoky heads amidst groves of palm trees; whilst iron railways intersected orange groves, and plantations of dates and pomegranates might be seen bordering excavations intended for coal pits. Colonies of English and Americans peopled the country, and produced a population that swarmed like bees over the land, and surpassed in numbers, even the wondrous throngs of the ancient Mizraim race; whilst industry and science changed desolation into plenty, and had converted barren plains into fertile kingdoms.

Amidst all these revolutions, however, the Pyramids still raised their gigantic forms, towering to the sky; unchanged, unchangeable, grand, simple, and immoveable, fit symbols of that majestic nature they were intended to represent, and seeming to look down with contempt upon the ephemeral structures with which they were surrounded; as though they would have said, had utterance been permitted to them – 'Avaunt, ye nothings of the day! Respect our dignity and sink into your original obscurity; for, know that we alone are monarchs of the plains.' Indestructible, however, as they had proved themselves, even their granite sides had not been able entirely to resist the corroding influence of the smoke with which they were now surrounded, and a slight crumbling announced the first outward symptom of decay.

Still, however, though blackened and disfigured, they shone stupendous monuments of former greatness; and Edric and his tutor gazed upon them with an awe that for some moments deprived them of utterance.

The doctor, however, who was too fond of reasoning ever long to remain willingly silent, after surveying them a few minutes, broke forth as follows: 'What noble piles! What majesty and grandeur they display in their formation, and yet what dignified simplicity! Can the imagination of man conceive anything more sublime than the thought that they have stood thus, frowning in awful magnificence, perhaps since the very creation of the world, without equals, without even competitors – mocking the feeble efforts of man to divine their origin, and seeing generation after generation pass away, whilst they still remain immutable, and involved in the same deep and unfathomable mystery as at first?'

'It is very strange,' observed Edric, 'that, in this age of speculation and discovery, nothing certain should be known concerning them.'

'It is,' returned the doctor: 'but the thick mysterious veil that has rested upon them for so many ages, seems not intended to be removed by mortal hands. They remind one of the sublime inscription upon the temple of the goddess, Isis, at Sais: "I am whatever was, whatever is, and whatever shall be; but no mortal has, as yet, presumed to raise the veil that covers me." '

'Your quotation is apt, doctor,' resumed Edric, 'for both relate to Nature. Indeed, Nature appears to be the deity which the ancient Egyptians worshipped, under all the various forms in which she presents herself; and their strange and animal deities were but reverenced as her symbols. It was Nature which they worshipped as Isis; it was Nature that was typified in the Pyramids; and the good taste of the Egyptians made them prefer the simple, the majestic, and the sublime, in those works which they destined to last for ages. Formerly, from the immensity of their population, and high state of their civilization, labour was so divided, and consequently so lightened, that multitudes were enabled to exist exempt from toil. These persons, devoting themselves to study, became *initiati*; and either enrolled themselves amongst the priesthood, or passed their lives in making themselves masters of the most abstract sciences. The consequences were natural: they followed up the ramifications of creation to their original source; they penetrated into the most profound secrets of Nature, and traced all her wonders in her works: aware, however, of the taste of the vulgar for anything above their comprehension, and of the natural craving of the human mind for mystery, they wrapped the discoveries they had made in a deep impenetrable veil, and concealed awful and sublime significations under the meanest and most disgusting images.'

'You are right,' said the doctor, 'in your observations upon the religion of the ancient Egyptians; but it does not appear to me that the Pyramids were erected by them.'

'What! I suppose you draw your conclusions from the want of hieroglyphics in their principal chambers; and, from what Herodotus says of their having been erected by a shepherd, you think they were the work of the Pallic race.'

'No; though I allow much may be said in favour of that hypothesis, particularly as Herodotus says the kings under whom they were erected, ordered all the Egyptian temples to be closed, which we know the shepherd or Pallic sovereigns did; but I cannot imagine that an ignorant, Goth-like race of shepherds, men accustomed to live in tents or in the open air, and possessing no talents but for war, were capable of constructing such immense piles. No, no, the Pyramids required gigantic conceptions, highly cultivated minds, and unwearied perseverance; all qualities quite incompatible with a warlike wandering race. I do not think the Palli were capable of imagining such structures, much less of constructing them. I think they were the work of evil spirits.'

'Evil spirits!' exclaimed Edric.

'Yes,' returned the doctor. 'We are told that the evil spirits, after their expulsion from Paradise, were under the command of the Sultan, or Soliman Giam ben Giam, as he is called by Arabic writers, but who is supposed to have been the same as Cheops; and I think that he employed them in this vast work.'

'I do not know by what analysis etymologists can draw the name of Cheops from that of Giam ben Giam" responded Edric, "but supposing the fact to be correct, that they designated the same person, I think it only proves more strongly my hypothesis; for the Palli came from Mount Caucasus, where the evil spirits were said to have been enchained, and if Cheops was a Pallic king, it is possible the Egyptians might poetically call their conquerors evil spirits.'

'That is a good idea, Edric; though I do not think it by any means certain that Cheops was a Pallic king. However, we shall soon be able to see his tomb, and judge for ourselves; for we have now approached near enough to the Pyramids to descend. Foh! what a smoke and what a noise! It is enough to rouse the mummies from their slumbers before their appointed time, and without the aid of galvanism. Have you opened the valves, Edric? Oh yes! I perceive we are getting lower; we will not lose a moment before we visit the Pyramid. But what a crowd of brutes are assembled to witness our arrival! They stare as though they had never seen a balloon before. Egypt is certainly a fine country, but the inhabitants are a century behind us in civilization.'

An immense crowd had gathered together to witness the descent of our travellers, and they did indeed stand staring, lost in stupid astonishment at the strange sight that presented itself; for though the Egyptian people had occasionally seen balloons, they had never before beheld one made of Indian rubber. The odd figure of the doctor, too, amused them exceedingly, as he sat wrapt up in the most dignified manner in an asbestos cloak, his bob-wig pushed a little on one side from the heat of the weather and the warmth of his argument; his round, red, oily face attempting to look solemn, and his little fat, punchy figure trying to assume an air of majesty. The Egyptians were amazingly struck with this apparition, and being, like most colonists, somewhat conceited and not very ceremonious in their manners, they looked at him a few minutes in silence, and then burst into immoderate fits of laughter.

The doctor was exceedingly indignant at this rude reception, and rising, shook his fist at them in anger; a manoeuvre that only redoubled the mirth of the unpolished Egyptians, whose peals of laughter now became so tremendous, that they actually shook the skies, and occasioned a most unpleasant vibration in the balloon. Edric, who was almost as much annoyed as the doctor, had yet sufficient self-command to continue calmly making preparations for his descent; and without taking the least notice of the crowd below, he screwed the top upon the propelling vapour-bottle; he let the inflammable air escape from the balloon, which rapidly collapsed as they approached the earth, and throwing out their patent spring grappling-irons, they caught one of the lower stones of the Great Pyramid, and in a few moments the car in which our travellers were sitting, was safely moored at a convenient distance from the earth for them to alight. Edric now unloosed the descending ladder, and reverentially assisted the doctor, who was encumbered with his long cloak, to reach terra firma in safety – amidst the bustle and exclamations of the crowd, who thronged round them, expressing their wonder and astonishment audibly, in broad English.

'Where the deuce did this spring from?' cried one; 'the car would load a waggon!'

'And what is gone with the balloon?' said another; 'it is clean vanished!'

'Well, I never saw such a thing in all my life before!' exclaimed a third; 'I think they must be come from the moon.'

'Hush! hush!' cried an old gentleman bustling amongst them, who seemed as one having authority. 'What's the matter? What's the matter?'

'We are strangers, Sir,' said Edric, advancing and addressing him. 'We come here to see the wonders of your country, and we wish to explore the Pyramids – but the reception we have met with –'

'Say no more – say no more!' interrupted the worthy justice, for such he was. 'Get about your business, you rapscallions, or I'll read the riot act! Here, Gregory, call out the *posse comitatus*, and set a guard of constables to keep watch over these gentlemen's balloon, whilst they go to explore the Pyramids. Eh, but where is the balloon? I don't see it. I hope neither of the gentlemen has put it in his pocket!' laughing at his own wit.

'No, Sir,' returned Edric, smiling, 'though it is a feat which might easily be accomplished, for that is our balloon,' pointing to the caoutchouc bottle, now shrunk to its original dimensions.

'Very strange, that!' said the justice; 'very curious, very curious indeed! Well, gentlemen, if you wish to proceed immediately, you'll want a guide of course. These cottages at the foot of the Pyramids are all inhabited by guides, who get their living by showing the sights. They are sad rogues, most of them, but I can recommend you to one who is a very honest man. Here, Samuel,' continued he, knocking against a small door, 'Samuel, I say!'

Samuel made his appearance, in the guise of a tall, raw-boned, stupid-looking fellow, with a pair of immensely broad stooping shoulders, which looked as though he could have relieved Atlas occasionally of his burthen, without much trouble to himself. Coming forth from his hut in an awkward shambling pace, he scratched his head, and demanded what his honour was pleased to want.

'You must show these gentlemen the Pyramids,' said the justice.

'Ay, that I will with pleasure!' returned Samuel. 'I've got my living by showing them these fifty years, man and boy; and I know every crink and cranny of them, though I'm old now and somewhat lame. So walk this way, gentlemen.'

'We are very much obliged to you, Sir,' said the doctor, bowing to the justice; who was in fact one of those good-natured, busy, bustling men, who are always better pleased to transact any other person's business than their own; and are never so happy as when a new arrival gives them an opportunity of showing off their consequence. Indeed, there is a pleasure in showing wonders to a stranger, that only those who have little else to occupy their minds can properly estimate: a man of this kind feels his self-love gratified by the superiority his local knowledge gives him over a stranger; and as it is, perhaps, the only chance he ever can have of showing superiority, they must be unreasonable who blame him for making the most of it. Justice Freemantle was accordingly exceedingly delighted with travellers who seemed disposed to submit implicitly to his dictation; and he returned a most gracious reply to the doctor's thanks.

'Don't mention it! Don't mention it, my dear Sir!' said he; 'I am never so happy as when I can make myself useful. Is there any thing else I can do for you? You may command me, I assure you; and you may depend upon it, no injury shall be done to your luggage, whilst you are away.'

'What a very civil, obliging, good-natured old gentleman!' said the doctor, as they walked towards the entrance of the Pyramids; 'I declare he almost reconciles me to the country, though, I own, I thought at first the people were the greatest brutes I had ever met with.'

'Which Pyramid does your honour wish to see?' asked the guide.

'That which contains the tomb of Cheops, man!' cried the doctor solemnly; who, encumbered with his long cloak, and loaded with his walking-stick and galvanic battery, had some difficulty in getting on.

'Won't your honour let me carry that pole and that box?' said the man; 'you'd get on a surprising deal better, if you would.'

'Avaunt, wretch!' exclaimed the doctor, 'nor offer to touch with thy profane fingers the immortal instruments of science.'

The man stared, but fell back, and the whole party walked

on in perfect silence.

In the mean time, Edric had advanced before his companions, completely lost in meditation. A crowd of conflicting thoughts rushed through his mind; and now, when he found himself at the very goal of his wishes, the daring nature of the purpose he had so long entertained, seemed to strike him for the first time, and he trembled at the consequences that might attend the completion of his desires. With his arms folded on his breast, he stood gazing on the Pyramids, whilst his ideas wandered uncontrolled through the boundless regions of space.

'And what am I,' thought he, 'weak, feeble worm that I am who dare seek to penetrate into the awful secrets of my Creator? Why should I wish to restore animation to a body now resting in the quiet of the tomb? What right have I to renew the struggles, the pains, the cares, and the anxieties of mortal life? How can I tell the fearful effects that may be produced by the gratification of my unearthly longing? May I not revive a creature whose wickedness may involve mankind in misery? And what if my experiment should fail, and if the moment when I expect my rash wishes to be accomplished, the hand of Almighty vengeance should strike me to the earth, and heap molten fire on my brain to punish my presumption!'

The sound of human voices, as the doctor and the guide

approached, grated harshly on the nerves of Edric, already overstrained by the awful nature of the thoughts in which he had been indulging, and he turned away involuntarily, to escape the interruption he dreaded, quite forgetting for the moment from whom the sounds most probably proceeded.

'Lord have mercy on us!' said the guide; 'I declare that gentleman looks as if he were beside himself; and see there if he hasn't walked right by the entrance to the Pyramid without seeing it! Sir! Sir!' halloed he.

Excessively annoyed, but recalled to his recollection by these shouts, Edric returned.

'These Pyramids are wonderful piles,' said the doctor, as he stumbled forward to meet him. 'I really had no adequate conception of the enormity of their size. They did not even look half so large at a distance as they do now.'

'Immense masses seldom do,' replied Edric, compelling himself with difficulty to speak.

'True,' returned the doctor; 'the simplicity and uniformity of their figures deceive the eyes, and it is only when we approach them that we feel their stupendous magnitude and our own insignificance!'

'They give an amazing idea of the grandeur of the ancient kings of Egypt,' said Edric, without exactly knowing what he was saying. 'Their palaces must have been superb, if they had such mausoleums.'

'How absurdly you reason, Edric!' replied the doctor peevishly; for, being annoyed with his burthens and his cloak, he was not in a humour to bear contradiction. 'I thought we had settled that question before. In the first place, I think it very doubtful whether the Egyptians had anything to do with the building of these monuments; and if they had, I believe they were meant for temples, not mausoleums; and in the next place, even if they were intended for tombs, their greatness affords no argument for the splendour of the surrounding palaces; as the Egyptians were celebrated for the superiority of their burying-places, and for the immense sums they expended upon them. Indeed, you know, ancient writers say they went so far as to call the houses of the living only inns, whilst they considered tombs as everlasting habitations – a circumstance, by the way, that strongly corroborates my hypothesis, at least as far as their opinions go; as it seems to imply that both soul and body were designed to remain there.'

They had now entered the Pyramid, and were proceeding with infinite difficulty along a low, dark, narrow passage.

'Observe, Edric,' said the doctor, 'how the difficulty and obscurity of these winding passages confirm my opinion: you know, the religion of the ancient Egyptians, like that of the ancient Hindoos, was one of penances and personal privations; and, granting that to be the case, what can be more simple than that the passages the *initiati* had to traverse before they reached the adytum, should be painful and difficult of access. Besides this, as, you know, the bones of a bull, no doubt those of the god Apis, were found in a sarcophagus in the second Pyramid, it seems probable that it was sacred to his worship: and its vicinity to the Nile, which was indispensable to the temples of Apis, as, when it was time for him to die, he was drowned in its waters, confirms the fact. Indeed, I am only surprised that any human being, possessing a grain of common sense, can entertain a single doubt upon the subject.'

'How do you account for the tomb we are about to visit being placed in the Pyramid, if you think they were only designed for temples?' asked Edric.

'The question is futile,' said the doctor. 'A strange fancy prevailed in former times, that burying the dead in consecrated places, particularly in temples intended for divine worship, would scare away the evil spirits, and the practice actually prevailed in England even as lately as the nineteenth or twentieth century. Indeed, it was not till after the country had been almost depopulated by the dreadfully infectious disease which prevailed about two hundred years ago, that a law was passed to prevent the interment of the dead in London, and that those previously buried in and near the churches there, were exhumed and placed in cemeteries beyond the walls.'

Edric did not reply, for in fact his ideas were so absorbed by the solemn object before him, that it was painful for him to speak, and the doctor's ill-timed reasoning created such an irritation of his nerves, that he found it required the utmost exertion of his self-command to endure it patiently. The passage they were traversing, now became higher and wider, shelving off occasionally into chambers or recesses on each side, till they approached a kind of vestibule, in the centre of which yawned a deep, dark, gloomy-looking cavity, like a well.

'We must descend that shaft,' said the guide, 'and that will lead us to the tomb of King Cheops; but as the road is dark, and rather dangerous, we had better, each of us, take a torch.'

As he spoke, he drew some torches from a niche where they were deposited, and began to illuminate them from his own. The red glare of the torches flashed fearfully on the massive walls of the Pyramid, throwing part of their enormous masses into deep shadow, as they rose in solemn and sublime dignity around, and seemed frowning upon the presumptuous mortals who had dared to invade their recesses, whilst the deep pit beneath their feet seemed to yawn wide to engulf them in its abyss. Edric's heart beat thick: it throbbed till he even fancied its pulsations audible;

and a strange, mysterious thrilling of anxiety, mingled with a wild, undefinable delight, ran through his frame. A few short hours, and his wishes would be gratified, or set at rest for ever. The doctor and the guide had already begun to descend, and their figures seemed changed and unearthly as the gleams of the torches fell upon them. Edric gazed for a moment, and then followed with feelings worked up almost to frenzy by the over-excitement of his nerves; whilst the hollow sounds that re-echoed from the walls, as they struck against them in their descent, thrilled through his whole frame.

No one spoke; and after proceeding for some time along the narrow path, or rather ledge, formed on the sides of the cavity, which gradually shelved downwards, the guide suddenly stopped, and touching a secret spring, a solid block of granite slowly detached itself from the wall, and, rising majestically like the portcullis of an ancient fortress, showed the entrance to a dark and dreary cave. The guide advanced, followed by our travellers, into a gloomy vaulted apartment, where longs vistas of ponderous arches stretched on every side, till their termination was lost in darkness, and gave a feeling of immensity and obscurity to the scene.

'I will wait here,' said the guide; 'and here, if you please, you had better leave your torches. That avenue will lead you to the tomb.'

The travellers obeyed; and the guide, placing himself in a recess in the wall, extinguished all the torches except one, which he shrouded so as to leave the travellers in total darkness. Nothing could be now more terrific than their situation: immured in the recesses of the tomb, involved in darkness, and their bosoms throbbing with hopes that they scarcely dared avow even to themselves; with faltering steps they proceeded slowly along the path the guide had pointed out, shuddering even at the hollow echo of their own footsteps, which alone broke the solemn silence that reigned throughout these fearful regions of terror and the tomb.

Suddenly, a vivid light flashed upon them, and, as they advanced, they found it proceeded from torches placed in the hands of two colossal figures, who, placed in a sitting posture, seemed guarding an enormous portal, surmounted by the image of a fox, the constant guardian of an Egyptian tomb. The immense dimensions and air of grandeur and repose about these colossi had something in it very imposing; and our travellers felt a sensation of awe creep over them as they gazed upon their calm unmoved features, so strikingly emblematic of that immutable nature which they were doubtless placed there to typify.

It was with feelings of indescribable solemnity, that the doctor and Edric passed through this majestic portal, and found themselves in an apartment gloomily illumined by the light shed faintly from an inner chamber, through ponderous brazen gates beautifully wrought. The light thus feebly emitted, showed that the room in which they stood was dedicated to Typhon, the evil spirit, as his fierce and savage types covered the walls; and images of his symbols, the crocodile and the dragon, placed beneath the shadow of the brazen gates, and dimly seen by the imperfect light, seemed starting into life, and grimly to forbid the farther advance of the intruders. Our travellers shuddered, and opening with trembling hand the ponderous gates, they entered the tomb of Cheops.

In the centre of the chamber, stood a superb, highly ornamented sarcophagus of alabaster, beautifully wrought: over this hung a lamp of wondrous workmanship, supplied by a potent mixture, so as to burn for ages unconsumed; thus awfully lighting up with perpetual flame the solemn mansions of the dead, and typifying life eternal even in the silent tomb. Around the room, on marble benches, were arranged mummies simply dried, apparently those of slaves; and close to the sarcophagus was placed one contained in a case, which the doctor approached to examine. This was supposed to be that of Sores, the confidant and prime-minister of Cheops. The chest that enclosed the body was splendidly ornamented with embossed gilt leather, whilst the parts not otherwise covered were stained with red and green curiously blended, and of a vivid brightness.

The mighty Phtah, the Jupiter of the Egyptians, spread its widely extended wings over the head, grasping in his monstrous claws a ring, the emblem of eternity; whilst below, the vulture-form of Rhea proclaimed the deceased a votary of that powerful deity; and on the sides were innumerable hieroglyphics. The doctor removed the lid, and shuddered as the crimson tinge of the everlasting lamp fell upon the hideous and distorted features thus suddenly exhibited to view. This sepulchral light, indeed, added unspeakable horror to the scene, and its peculiar glare threw such a wild and demoniac expression on the dark lines and ghastly lineaments of the mummies, that even the doctor felt his spirits depressed, and a supernatural dread creep over his mind as he gazed upon them.

In the mean time, Edric had stood gazing upon the sarcophagus of Cheops, the sides of which were beautifully sculptured with groups of figures, which, from the peculiar light thrown upon them, seemed to possess all the force and reality of life. On one side was represented an armed and youthful warrior bearing off in his arms a beautiful female, on whom he gazed with the most passionate fondness. He was pursued by a crowd of people and soldiers, who seemed to be rending the air with vehement exclamations against his violence, and endeavouring in vain to arrest his progress; whilst in the background appeared an old man, who was tearing his hair and wringing his hands in ineffectual rage against the ravisher.

The other side presented the same old man wrestling with the youthful warrior, who had just overpowered and stabbed him; the helpless victim raising his withered hands and failing eyes to Heaven as he fell, as though to implore vengeance upon his murderer, whilst the crimson current was fast ebbing from his bosom. The dying look and agony of the old man were forcibly depicted, whilst upon the features of the youthful warrior glowed the fury of a demon.

The sarcophagus was supported by the lion, emblem of royalty, the symbol of the solar god Horus; and above it sat the majestic hawk of Osiris, gazing upwards, and unmindful of the subtle crocodile of Typhon, that, crouching under its feet, was just about to seize its breast in its enormous jaws. Neither of the travellers had as yet spoken, for it seemed like sacrilege to disturb the awful stillness that prevailed even by a whisper. Indeed, the solemn aspect of the chamber thrilled through every nerve, and they moved slowly, gliding along with noiseless steps as though they feared prematurely to break the slumbers of the mighty dead it contained. They gazed, however, with deep, but undefinable interest upon the sculptured mysteries of the tomb of Cheops, vainly endeavouring to decipher their meaning; whilst, as they found their efforts useless, a secret voice seemed to whisper in their bosoms – 'And shall finite creatures like these, who cannot even explain the signification of objects presented before their eyes, presume to dive into the mysteries of their Creator's will? Learn wisdom by this omen, nor seek again to explore secrets above your comprehension! Retire, whilst it is yet time; soon it will be too late!'

Edric started at his own thoughts, as the fearful warning, 'soon it will be too late,' rang in his ears; and a fearful presentiment of evil weighed heavily upon his soul. He turned to look upon the doctor, but he had already seized the lid of the sarcophagus, and, with a daring hand, removed it from its place, displaying in the fearful light the royal form that lay beneath. For a moment, both Edric and the doctor paused, not daring to survey it; and when they did, they both uttered an involuntary cry of astonishment, as the striking features of the mummy met their eyes, for both instantly recognized the sculptured warrior in his traits. Yes, it was indeed the same, but the fierce expression of fiery and ungoverned passions depicted upon the countenance of the marble figure, had settled down to a calm, vindictive and concentrated hatred upon that of its mummy prototype in the tomb.

Awful, indeed, was the gloom that sat upon that brow,

and bitter the sardonic smile that curled those haughty lips. All was perfect as though life still animated the form before them, and it had only reclined there to seek a short repose. The dark eyebrows, the thick raven hair which hung upon the forehead, and the snow-white teeth seen through the half-open lips, forbade the idea of death; whilst the fiend-like expression of the features made Edric shudder, as he recollected the purpose that brought him to the tomb, and he trembled at the thought of awakening such a fearful being from the torpor of the grave to all the renewed energies of life.

'Let us go,' whispered the doctor to his pupil, in a low, deep, and unearthly tone, fearfully different from his usually cheerful voice. Edric started at the sound, for it seemed the last sad warning of his better genius, before it abandoned him for ever. The die, however, was cast, and it was too late to recede. Edric felt worked up to frenzy by the over-wrought feelings of the moment. He seized the machine, and resolutely advanced towards the sarcophagus, whilst the doctor gazed upon him with a horror that deprived him of either speech or motion.

Innumerable folds of red and white linen, disposed alternately, swathed the gigantic limbs of the royal mummy; and upon his breast lay a piece of metal, shining like silver, and stamped with the figure of a winged globe. Edric attempted to remove this, but recoiled with horror, when he found it bend beneath his fingers with an unnatural softness; whilst, as the flickering light of the lamp fell upon the face of the mummy, he fancied its stern features relaxed into a ghastly laugh of scornful mockery. Worked up to desperation, he applied the wires of the battery and put the apparatus in motion, whilst a demoniac laugh of derision appeared to ring in his ears, and the surrounding mummies seemed starting from their places and dancing in unearthly merriment. Thunder now roared in tremendous peals through the Pyramids, shaking their enormous masses to the foundation, and vivid flashes of light darted round in quick succession.

Edric stood aghast amidst this fearful convulsion of nature. A horrid creeping seemed to run through every vein, every nerve feeling as though drawn from its extremity, and wrapped in icy chillness round his heart. Still, he stood immoveable, and gazing intently on the mummy, whose eyes had opened with the shock, and were now fixed on those of Edric, shining with supernatural lustre. In vain Edric attempted to rouse himself; in vain to turn away from that withering glance. The mummy's eyes still pursued him with their ghastly brightness; they seemed to possess the fabled fascination of those of the rattle-snake, and though he shrank from their gaze, they still glared horribly upon him. Edric's senses swam, yet he could not move from the spot; he remained fixed, chained, and immoveable, his eyes still riveted upon those of the mummy, and every thought absorbed in horror.

Another fearful peal of thunder now rolled in lengthened vibrations above his head, and the mummy rose slowly, his eyes still fixed upon those of Edric, from his marble tomb. The thunder pealed louder and louder. Yells and groans seemed mingled with its roar; the sepulchral lamp, flared with redoubled fierceness, flashing its rays around in quick succession, and with vivid brightness; whilst by its horrid and uncertain glare, Edric saw the mummy stretch out its withered hand, as though to seize him. He saw it rise gradually – he heard the dry, bony fingers rattle as it drew them forth – he felt its tremendous grip – human nature could bear no more – his senses were rapidly deserting him; he felt, however, the fixed, steadfast eyes of Cheops still glowing upon his failing orbs, as the lamp gave a sudden flash, and then all was darkness! The brazen gates now shut with a fearful clang, and Edric, uttering a shriek of horror, fell senseless upon the ground, whilst his shrill cry of anguish rang wildly through the marble vaults, till its re-echoes seemed like the yell of demons joining in fearful mockery.

How long he lay in this state he knew not; but when he re-opened his eyes, for the moment, he fancied all that had passed a dream. As his senses returned he recollected where he was, and shuddered to find himself yet in that place of horrors. All now was dark, except a faint gleam that shone feebly through the half-open gates; these ponderous portals slowly unclosed, and the form of a man, wrapped in a large cloak, and bearing a torch, entered, peering around as it advanced, as though half afraid to proceed. Edric's feelings were too highly wrought to bear any fresh horrors, and he shrieked in agony as the figure approached. The sound of his voice subdued the terrors of the intruder, and the doctor, for it was he, shouted with joy, as he rushed forward to embrace him.

'Edric! Edric! thank God he is alive!' exclaimed he. 'Edric! My beloved Edric! for God's sake, let us leave this den of horrors! Come, come!'

Reassured by his tutor's voice, Edric arose, and taking one hasty, shuddering glance around as the light gleamed on the sarcophagus, he hurried out of the tomb. Neither he nor the doctor spoke as they passed through the vestibule, where the colossal figures still sat in awful majesty; indeed, as their torches were extinguished, their gigantic forms looked still more terrific than before, from the wavering and indistinct light thrown upon them. Edric shuddered as he looked, and hurried on with hasty strides to the place where they had left the guide, whom they found kneeling in a corner, hiding his face in his hands, and roaring out, 'O Lord, defend us!

Heaven have mercy upon us! Lord have mercy upon us! Heaven have mercy upon us!'

'He has been in that state for more than an hour,' said the doctor mournfully, 'for, after I came to myself, I tried to rouse him, but all to no purpose.'

'Then you also fainted?' said Edric, with difficulty compelling himself to speak.

'Why,' resumed the doctor with some hesitation, 'I don't know that you can exactly call it fainting; but the fact was, when I saw you touch the plate upon the mummy's breast, and start back, looking so horribly frightened, I – I thought I had better call for assistance; so as I ran for that purpose; somehow or other I fell down, and lay insensible I don't know how long. When I came to myself, I tried to rouse the guide, and when I found I could not, I came to seek you. But now that we are both recovered, I really don't know what is to become of us; for this fellow will never be able to show us the way out, and I'm sure I don't know the road.'

'Let us try to find it, at any rate,' said Edric faintly.

'Oh, for God's sake, take me too!' screamed the guide. 'If you have any mercy, don't leave me in this fearful place.'

'Take the light then, and lead the way,' said Edric. The guide obeyed, shaking in every limb, and every now and then casting a terrified look behind, whilst the quivering flame of the torch betrayed the unsteadiness of the trembling hands that bore it. In this manner they proceeded, starting at every sound, and frightened even at their own shadows, without daring to stop till they reached the plain.

'Thank God!' cried the doctor, the moment they stepped out of the Pyramid; looking round him, gasping for breath, and inhaling the fresh air with rapture.

'Thank God!' reiterated Edric and the guide, as they walked rapidly towards the place where they had left their balloon. When arrived there, however, they looked for it in vain; and fancying themselves under the influence of a delusion, they rubbed their eyes, and again looked, but without success.

'Dear me, it is very strange!' said the doctor; 'this is certainly the place, and yet, where can it be?'

'Where, indeed!' repeated Edric, 'horrors and unaccountable incidents environ us at every step; I am not naturally timid, yet –'

'Ah!' screamed the doctor, as he tumbled over a man lying with his face upon the ground. 'Oh!' groaned he, as Edric and the guide with difficulty raised him; 'would to Heaven I were safe at home again in my own comfortable little study, indulging in pleasing anticipations of that, which I find is any thing in the world but pleasing in reality.'

The mummy thus strangely recalled to life, was indeed Cheops! And horrible were the sensations that throbbed through every nerve as returning consciousness brought with it all the pangs of his former existence, and renewed circulation thrilled through every vein. His first impulse was to quit the tomb in which he had been so long immured, and seek again the regions of light and day. Instinct seemed to guide him to this; for, as yet, a mist hung over his faculties, and ideas thronged in painful confusion through his mind, which he was incapable of either arranging or analysing.

When, however, he reached the plain, light and air seemed to revive him and restore his scattered senses; and, gazing wildly around, he exclaimed, 'Where am I? what place is this? Methinks all seems wondrous, new, and strange! Where is my father? And where! oh, where, is my Arsinöe? Alas, alas!' continued he wildly; 'I had forgotten – I hoped it was a dream, a fearful dream, for methinks I have been long asleep. Was it, indeed, reality? Are all, all gone? And was that hideous scene true? – Those horrors, which still haunt my memory like a ghastly vision? Speak! speak!' continued he, his voice rising in thrilling energy as he spoke, 'Speak! let me hear the sound of another's voice, before my brain is lost in madness. Have I entered Hades, or am I still on earth? – yes, yes, it is still the earth, for there the mighty Pyramid I caused to be erected towers behind me. Yet where is Memphis? Where are my forts and palaces? What a dark, smoky mass of buildings now surrounds me! Can this be the once proud Queen of Cities? I see no palaces, no temples

– Memphis is fallen. The mighty barrier that protected her splendour from the waste of waters, must have been swept away by the encroaching inroads of the swelling Nile. But is this the Nile?' continued he, looking wildly upon the river; 'sure I must be deceived. It is the fatal river of the dead. No papyrine boats glide smoothly on its surface; but strange, infernal vessels, vomiting forth volumes of fire and smoke. Holy Osiris, defend me! Where am I? Where have I been? A misty veil seems thrown upon the face of nature. Awake, awake!' cried he, with a scream of agony; 'set me free; I did not mean to slay him!'

Then throwing himself violently upon the ground, he lay for some moments, apparently insensible. Then slowly rising, he looked at himself, and a deep, unnatural shuddering convulsed his whole frame. His sensations of identity became confused, and he recoiled with horror from himself: 'These are the trappings of a mummy!' murmured he in a hollow whisper. 'Am I then dead?' The next instant, however, he broke into a wild laugh of derision — 'Poor, feeble wretch!' cried he; 'what do I fear? – Need *I* tremble, in whose bosom dwells everlasting fire? Let me rather rejoice. I cannot be more wretched; why should I dread a change? I welcome it with transport, and dare my future fate.'

At this moment the car of the balloon caught his eye: 'Ah! what is that?' cried he; 'I am summoned! 'Tis the boat of

Hecate, ready to ferry me across the Maerian Lake, to learn my final doom. I come! I come! I fear no judgment! *My hell is here!*' and, striking his bosom, he leaped into the car, and stamped violently against its sides.

At this instant Gregory awoke, and his terror was not surprising. The dried distorted features of the mummy looked yet more hideous than before, when animated by human passions, and his deep hollow voice, speaking in a language he did not understand, fell heavily upon his ear, like the groans of fiends. Gregory tried to scream, but he could not utter a sound. He attempted to fly, but his feet seemed nailed to the spot on which he stood, and he remained with his eyes fixed upon the mummy, gasping for breath, while a cold sweat distilled from every pore. In the mean time, Cheops had stumbled over the box containing the apparatus for making inflammable air, and striking it violently, had unintentionally set the machinery in motion. The pipes, tubes, and bellows, instantly began to work; and the Indian-rubber bottle became gradually inflated, till it swelled to an enormous magnitude, and fluttered in the air like an imprisoned bird, beating itself against the massive walls to which it was still attached.

'Still it goes not,' cried Cheops, again stamping impatiently. The quicksilver vapour bottle had fallen beneath his feet, and it broke as he trod upon it. The vapour burst from it with inconceivable violence, and tearing the balloon from its fastenings, sent it off through the air, like an arrow darting from a bow.

www.ingramcontent.com/pod-product-compliance
Lightning Source LLC
Chambersburg PA
CBHW022156260626
47155CB00018B/2270